The most remarkable aspects of nature range from the terrifying to the beautiful, but all of them are fascinating. Here are some possible explanations of both causes and effects as far as they are known.

Acknowledgments
The authors and publishers wish to acknowledge the use of photographs and other illustrative material as follows: pages 21, 47 (inset)—Camera Press; cover, front endpaper, and pages 4, 6, 7 (top), 11 (bottom), 14, 20 (both), 26, 27, 29, 31, 35, 37 (both), 40, 47, 49, 51 (both)—Bruce Coleman Ltd; pages 8, 12 (inset), 23, 34, 38, 39, 43, 46—Colour Library International Ltd; pages 18/19—P J Cutting; page 23—J H Golden; page 48—Hansen Planetarium, Utah; page 28—J Leigh-Pemberton; page 50—Mansell Collection Ltd; page 16—NASA; pages 12/13—Visnews; title page and page 24—G Witcomb; pages 17, 33—Diana Wyllie Ltd.

Volcanoes
and other natural phenomena

by Robin *and* Muriel McCurdy
illustrations by Keith Logan

Ladybird Books

Most animals adapt to the world they live in. People try to adapt that world to their needs—and often succeed. But as smart as people are, there are some things they cannot control. Some things in nature are frightening in their very power, such as earthquakes and volcanoes. And there are things such as icebergs, lurking dangerously in wait.

One of the things man would *like* to control is the weather—too little or too much rain can ruin a harvest, which means that people will go hungry; lightning can kill people; and high winds can damage homes.

The damage an earthquake can do:
Guatemala City, in Central America

Rain

A very heavy rainfall is called a *deluge*. Most people have heard of the deluge that brought about Noah's Flood. In the Bible it says, "And the rain was upon the Earth forty days and forty nights." Later it goes on, "Everything died that had the breath of life in its nostrils, everything on dry land. God wiped out every living thing that existed on Earth, man and beast, reptile and bird; they were all wiped out over the whole Earth, and only Noah and his company in the ark survived."

We don't know for certain that Noah's Flood really happened, but we do know that many of the world's peoples have a story about a deluge of this kind as part of their tradition. It is a way of showing that a new start took place in the lives of the people at that time. It may also show a change in their way of thinking. The flood causes death, and from the waters life comes once more.

The story of Noah closely resembles a far older Babylonian story of Utnapishtim, told in the great epic of Gilgamesh. This in turn was based on the Sumerian legend of Ziusudra. In Hindu mythology, the god Vishnu appears to Manu, the first man, in the form of a fish and warns him of the coming flood. Then Vishnu himself leads Manu's ship to a safe mooring in the mountains of the north.

Unfortunately, deluges and floods are not just part of history. They still happen. Sometimes heavy rain can cause a sudden, violent flood down a hillside. This is called a *flash flood*. Although it does not last long, it can ruin both crops and homes in the river valley below. Following a freak storm in north Devon, England, in 1952, the town of Lynmouth was struck by such a flood. Twenty-eight bridges and nearly a hundred houses were damaged or destroyed, and thirty-one lives were lost.

Flash flooding on a hillside in Ecuador, South America

To minimize among other things the disastrous effects of flash flooding, hillsides are terraced in many parts of the world. For the same reason, farmers often plow around the curve of a hill, instead of up and down; this system, shown opposite, is called contour plowing.

Severe flooding in the Severn Valley, England, in 1981

Where there are mountains and plateaus, the rainfall is often heavy. This is because as air rises, it cools and can hold less moisture. The moisture then falls as rain. The rainiest spot in England is Borrowdale, in the county of Cumbria in the northwest, where 165 inches of rain fall each year. On the other hand, parts of eastern England have less than 20 inches a year. A really heavy rainfall of over 600 inches a year has been recorded in the foothills of the Himalayas.

Rainbows

For people everywhere and in every time, the rainbow has always symbolized hope.

Rainbows appear in showery weather, and each round raindrop acts as a tiny prism. The sun's rays are first *refracted* (bent) as they enter the raindrop. Then they are reflected from the raindrop's far surface. Finally they are refracted once more as they pass out. The result is that the light rays are broken up into the spectrum of colors—red, orange, yellow, green, blue, indigo, and violet—that we see in the form of a rainbow.

A rainbow is really part of a circle, the center of which is as far below the horizon as the sun is above it. Sometimes you may even see two rainbows at the same time, one inside the other.

Although today the rainbow holds no mystery for us, its beauty still has the power to make us wonder.

Drought

When there is little or no rain for a long time, this is called a *drought*. In Britain, an "absolute drought" is considered to be a period of at least fifteen days on which the rainfall each day has been not more than 0.01 inches.

Since Britain's climate is not normally dry, a drought can create unexpected problems. Besides making it necessary to limit the use of water, for example, a long dry period can dry out the subsoil, which then cracks. Buildings may then begin to *subside* (sink) because their weight can no longer be supported. This is especially true of buildings near large trees, because the trees' roots are drawing out what little water is left in the soil (as shown below).

Snow, hail, and fog

Although we like to think of a "white Christmas" as traditional, it doesn't happen very often in Britain. In the southern half of the country, it has only snowed on Christmas Day six times in 83 years!

In the British Isles, snow falls more often toward the end of the winter and the early part of the spring. At that time of year, easterly winds are more likely to bring cold weather from Europe. The county of Kent has more than its fair share of snowstorms just *because* it is nearest to the continent.

Sometimes people say that it is "too cold for snow." Strictly speaking, it can never be too cold to snow. In Britain, however, there is some truth to the saying, for when the temperature falls very low, it is usually during an *anticyclone*, or period of settled weather. At these times there is not likely to be much *precipitation* (rain, hail, or snow) at all, of any kind. With the approach of a *depression*, or low-pressure area, the temperature may rise as the snow comes nearer. This is especially true if it comes from the continent, bringing an easterly wind on its northern edge.

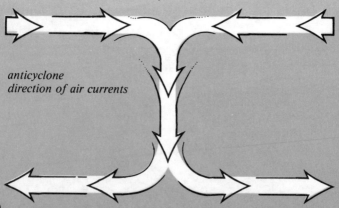

*anticyclone
direction of air currents*

If you look at a large hailstone carefully, you may find that it looks something like an onion, with alternate layers of hard clear ice and soft opaque ice. The layers are created when frozen raindrops fall a short distance, then are carried up again to the colder layers of air. Sometimes, as in thunderstorms, this may happen several times before they finally fall to Earth. In this way, hailstones may build up to a considerable

The layers of a hailstone

size. When they fall, they can shatter glass and even fracture human skulls.

In 1983, hailstones weighing as much as six pounds fell in China, killing a number of people. Even in Britain hailstones as big as golf balls have fallen. In thunderstorms, the greatest danger to aircraft is not the lightning. It is the powerful up-currents within the thunderclouds and the possible bombardment by hailstones, which can puncture the airplane's fuselage.

Hailstones, magnified

11

Early morning mist at Godalming, Surrey, in England

Snow and fog are also dangerous to aircraft. In a severe blizzard, for example, visibility can be reduced to zero.

We can predict where fog may appear. It may occur in lowlands on cold, clear nights, and on uplands in the form of low cloud. On a cloudless night, the air near the ground cools rapidly as it loses heat gained during the day. If the air cools to the *dew point* (the temperature at which moist air will deposit the water in it as dew), dew begins to settle on the ground. Some of the water vapor above the ground may condense in tiny droplets, and these remain in the air as fog. Because cold air is heavier than warm air, such fog tends to lie in valleys and hollows.

More widespread fog forms when warm, moist air passes over colder land or water. Coastal fogs are of this type and may occur at any time of year. They are really clouds that form on the Earth's surface, and they are hardly ever more than 200 feet thick.

In many urban areas, a very dense fog made up of fog and smoke may form under certain conditions. It is known as *smog*. In the memorable London smog of 1952, doctors thought that the weather was responsible for about 4,000 deaths. Even animals appeared to be affected. Nowadays, with the advent of smokeless fuels and a greater use of electricity, there is much less smog in London.

Smog in Tokyo, Japan

Storms and hurricanes

Throughout the world, something like 45,000 storms are recorded every day. They are nature's way of restoring the balance of the atmosphere, by releasing excess energy.

Every year, at least twelve *hurricanes* start in the Atlantic Ocean. The word hurricane comes from a West Indian word meaning "big wind." For a hurricane to come into existence, the temperature of the sea has to be at least 80°F. This means that the cooler parts of the Earth rarely get hurricanes.

Two factors combine in the formation of a hurricane: a core of warm air near the sea, and special conditions in the atmosphere above. As the warm moist air rises, it is distributed by high-level winds blowing outward. This reduces pressure at sea level. Air rushes into this low-pressure center, the Earth's rotation gives a twist to the column of rising air, and a hurricane *vortex* is born. (A vortex is a rapidly spiraling column of air.) Winds that are drawn into the vortex may reach speeds of 150 – 200 miles an hour, and can cause damage over an

Damage caused by a hurricane in Vanuatu, in the South Pacific Ocean

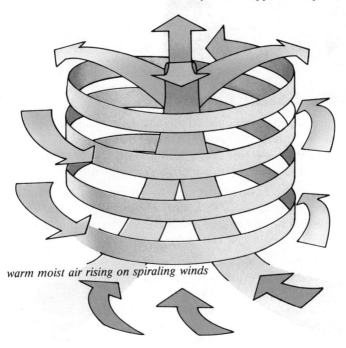

anticyclone in upper atmosphere

warm moist air rising on spiraling winds

cool air rushing into the area of low pressure

area as great as 400 miles in diameter.

In the center of the system is the calm but menacing *eye* of the storm, which is comparatively quiet and still. It is probably about 20 miles across. As the eye passes, the howling, screaming winds start once more. This time, however, they blow in an opposite direction, leaving a wide trail of destruction.

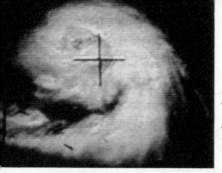

Hurricane Daisy as seen from a satellite. This photograph shows the revolving movement of the hurricane very clearly.

Once inland, hurricanes seldom last more than a day. This is because over land the things that keep the hurricane going (the heat, moisture, and low *drag*, or resistance over the surface of the sea) are all lost.

Torrential rain often accompanies hurricanes and thunderstorms. In 1954, a hurricane called Alice poured 27 inches of rain over southwest Texas—more rain than falls in a whole year in London.

Hurricanes can do great damage both to shipping at sea and to buildings and crops on land. In 1900, in Galveston, Texas, a hurricane created storm tides that swept 6,000 people to their deaths. Over half a million people in Bangladesh were killed by a surge of water that followed a tropical storm in the Bay of Bengal in 1970.

Hurricane is not the only word for a tropical revolving storm. In the West Pacific such storms are called *typhoons*, and in Australian waters they are known by the aboriginal name of *willy-willy*.

A *tornado*—from the Spanish word *tornar*, "to twist or turn"—is also a column of swiftly spinning air. However, it is much narrower, sometimes only a few hundred yards across.

Tornadoes tend to occur on hot, humid days, mostly in the central areas of the United States, but also in the China Sea, the Bay of Bengal, the West Indies, the South Pacific, and Australia. No one knows just how tornadoes are formed, but they can sometimes be predicted. First seen as a downward-spiraling growth from a cloud, a tornado moves forward at a speed of up to 40 miles an hour. When the snaking, twisting cloud reaches the ground, it arrives with a deafening roar of upsurging winds. The atmospheric pressure drops, creating what is almost a vacuum. Since this means that the pressure inside buildings, for example, is much greater than that outside, windowpanes are sucked outward, corks are drawn from bottles, and buildings may explode.

The wind speed at the center of a tornado has been estimated at more than 400 miles an hour. Objects as big as cars and houses are swept up into the air, and the path in the wake of a tornado looks like a battlefield. Torrential rain pours down as the column brings destruction to everything it touches.

Tornado over Texas

17

Lightning and thunder

About 1,800 thunderstorms are happening at
any given moment in various parts of the world.
They occur in both temperate and tropical
regions. For a thunderstorm to develop,
there must be strongly rising currents of
warm air, so such storms occur most often
in summer. As the warm air cools, the
moisture it contains condenses, and forms
the cauliflowerlike *cumulus* clouds that
are often seen just before a storm. They
may rise to an altitude of some 20,000 feet.

In scientific terms, lightning is a gigantic
electrical spark. When such a giant spark
leaps from one part of a thundercloud to
another, it appears as *sheet* lightning.
(Reflections in the sky of lightning
flashes far beyond the horizon
are also called sheet lightning.)
A spark between cloud and ground
produces *forked* lightning.

Because thunderclouds contain a great deal
of water and have strong up-currents, they act
as generators and produce electrical charges.
If a cloud has a heavy positive charge it
will discharge it to the ground. Sometimes
the flash may be within the cloud itself,
if the top and bottom of the cloud have
different charges, negative and positive.
This is like the spark you get if you
accidentally connect the two terminals
of a battery. Air is a good *insulator*—
it usually keeps electricity from
passing through. So a tremendous
voltage has to build up before
the insulating effect of the
air is broken down and the
electricity is discharged.
That voltage can be
as high as one
billion volts.

Considering how many thunderstorms there are, surprisingly few people are killed by them: in Britain the yearly average is 11 people. Both trees and buildings, however, are struck and damaged by lightning. This is why you should never seek shelter under a tree during a thunderstorm.

In ancient times lightning, like the sun's rays, was regarded as creative as well as destructive. We now know that this is true, because lightning causes nitrogen and oxygen in the air to combine and form nitrates. These dissolve in rain and fall to Earth, providing a form of fertilizer for plant life.

Trees struck by lightning

Thunder is really the sound of air exploding. The lightning flash heats the surrounding air so much that it expands and explodes. The temperature can be three times hotter than the surface of the sun!

Lightning travels to Earth at the speed of light— 186,000 miles per *second*—and the sound of thunder travels along at a mere 12 miles a *minute*. So it is possible to estimate how far away a storm is. A five-second delay between flash and sound represents about one mile.

Lightning may have helped to start life on this planet. As an experiment, an electrical charge was passed through a mixture of the gases believed to have been present in Earth's early atmosphere. This was found to produce complex chemicals known as *amino acids*, which are the basic building blocks of all forms of life.

Fireballs, or ball lightning, are a rare form of lightning seen occasionally on high trees, lightning conductors, or the masts of ships.

The path of a fireball

Waterspouts and dust storms

When a tornado runs over water, powerful up-currents of warm air are created, and a *waterspout* is formed. The bottom of the column sucks water up into the base of the whirling funnel.

Waterspouts are strong enough to suck up small creatures such as frogs as well, which then come down with the rain that follows. Small boats may be sunk or severely damaged, or sailors washed overboard, in the violent wind and rain that accompanies waterspouts.

Waterspout in Florida

Dust storm

In Britain, loose sand is sometimes driven by the wind along a dry beach. After a spell of dry weather, too, the wind will raise clouds of dust from plowed fields. Indeed, where hedgerows and belts of trees have been uprooted to provide more space, soil erosion by the wind is becoming a serious problem. This is the case in the flat counties of East Anglia, where crops are sometimes severely damaged.

Dust storms occur in arid regions such as deserts where there are no mountains or other barriers to the wind. They produce a scorching, suffocating blast that blots out the sun and carries loose debris and sand over great distances. They will even carry sand over water, for there are sand dunes in the Canary Islands, off the northwestern coast of Africa, made of sand blown from the Sahara Desert.

Sometimes in the desert, or in a hot dusty street in a city like Cairo, a miniature whirlwind will produce columnlike spirals of dust hurrying over the ground. They are quite unpredictable and can be a nuisance. They are known as "dust devils."

The oceans

The watery planet

No one yet knows how this planet Earth was formed, nor exactly how old it is. Scientists believe that more than four billion years ago, the Earth was a whirling mass of flaming gases. Slowly the mass cooled and condensed. First it became liquid, then semiliquid, and finally took solid form.

As the fiery Earth cooled, a great cloud of vapor hung over it. The surface was so hot that any moisture falling on it changed at once back into vapor, and rose again.

At last, when the Earth's crust had cooled sufficiently, the rain fell. It rained all day and every day, for many hundreds of years, filling the great hollows of the Earth.

In this way our oceans and seas came into being, and seven-tenths of the planet was covered with water.

At first the seas were probably only a little salty. Then rivers, flowing down the mountains and across the plains, brought rocks and minerals and salts from the land. The seas grew saltier—and have been growing saltier ever since.

When we measure the height of a mountain, it is measured from "sea level." This, however, is an average of the ocean levels, because the sea isn't really level at all.

Tides are produced by two gigantic bulges of water passing around the Earth as it rotates. They are on opposite sides of the Earth, and are called *antipodal bulges*. They are really very long, low waves produced mainly by the pull of the moon and, to a lesser extent, the sun.

Sometimes, when a powerful tidal current flows through an irregular channel, or when two currents meet, a violent circular eddy occurs. This is called a *maelstrom* —a Norwegian word meaning "whirling stream."

Tidal bulges

An iceberg in Greenland

Polar regions

From the North Pole, every direction is south. The heart of the region is the Arctic Ocean, much of which is covered year-round with pack ice.

The huge floating islands of ice are called *ice floes*. In winter, they close up and pile on top of one another, and then the ice may be up to 200 feet thick. But the sea below never freezes, and submarines have traveled to the North Pole beneath the ice. Seals and millions of sea birds thrive on the marine life of the Arctic Ocean.

Although the lands fringing that ocean are cold, they are really deserts, because they have less than 10 inches of rain each year. Even so, in the short summer, the landscape is full of color and movement. Migratory animals such as reindeer and musk ox feed on the lichens and sedges. They in turn are followed by predators such as polar bears and arctic foxes. In the long winter, with its almost perpetual night, nearly all activity comes to a complete halt.

A young polar bear on pack ice in the Arctic Circle

While the Arctic is an ocean, Antarctica is a huge continent at the other end of the Earth. It is half again as large as the United States, covered by an icecap that is sometimes nearly 10,000 feet thick. Like the Arctic, it is in darkness for six months of the year.

Most of Antarctica is mountainous. The South Pole itself is 9,070 feet above sea level, and in places the great ice plateau rises to more than 14,000 feet. For this reason it is much colder than the Arctic. Even in summer temperatures remain below the freezing point, and average winter temperatures are the world's lowest. In 1960 a record −126°F was recorded at the Russian base Vostok.

The Antarctic Ocean, some of it covered with pack ice and swept by bitter winds, is the stormiest place in the world. It is, however, rich in the microscopic marine life called *plankton*. One species of plankton, the krill, is the food of the world's largest mammal, the 100-ton blue whale. Fish too feed on the plankton, and they in turn are preyed upon by penguins and seals. Antarctica itself has practically no plant life.

Blue whale

*Iceberg in
the Ross Sea, in
the Antarctic Circle*

The Antarctic is an intensely interesting
region for scientists, who study the ice and its
effects on the rest of the world. Over the last hundred
years, there has been a worldwide melting of ice.
Glaciers and icecaps have shrunk, and the average sea
level has risen three inches since 1880. If all the
Antarctic ice were to melt, low-lying cities like New
York, Tokyo, and London would be flooded.

Icebergs

One of water's unique qualities is that it floats when frozen. This is because it expands as it freezes and becomes less dense. On land, the force of this expansion can crack rocks, and helps in the weathering process that produces soil.

In polar regions, huge ice floes form, covering the surfaces of lakes and oceans with a protective blanket. This prevents further freezing, so that life can go on in the waters underneath. More than three-quarters of the

Iceberg calving

world's fresh water is locked in the polar icecaps. If only a small fraction of this could be transported, it could be used to transform the arid deserts of the world, making them fertile and productive.

Over many thousands of years in the valleys of Antarctica in the south and Greenland in the north, compressed snow has gradually turned to ice, and has formed *glaciers*, which move slowly down to the sea. In the North Atlantic about 16,000 icebergs, some many miles in extent, are "calved" each year, mostly from glaciers along the shores of Greenland. The icebergs float slowly away, borne by ocean currents, until they gradually melt and disappear.

Because ice is only a little lighter than water, there is about eight times as much ice below the surface as there is above the surface. Icebergs therefore pose a great danger to shipping. An iceberg was the cause of a shipping disaster that shook the world. On April 14, 1912, a splendid new luxury liner called the *Titanic* was on her maiden voyage from England to America when she rammed an iceberg. Although she was believed to be unsinkable, she sank in less than three hours, and more than 1,500 people drowned.

Mendenhall Glacier, in Alaska

The aurora

In the northern hemisphere, these beautiful and awe-inspiring lights are called the *aurora borealis*, or *northern lights*. In the southern hemisphere they are called the *aurora australis*.

Although their full magnificence is seldom seen outside the polar regions, they are sometimes seen in the northern United States. No one can tell when such a display is likely to happen.

The real mystery of this phenomenon has not yet been solved by scientists. It is possibly created in much the same way as pictures on a television screen. Electrically charged particles (probably originating from the sun) travel downward in streams carrying almost equal numbers of positive and negative charges. They are focused by the Earth's magnetic field onto the "screen" of the sky above the poles—just as the beam of electrons is focused onto the fluorescent television screen by electromagnets.

The magnetic fields at the poles are funnel-shaped, and it is thought that as the particles spiral down they excite atoms in the upper air. Oxygen atoms produce the red, yellow, and green lights, and nitrogen the violet and blue lights, of the *aurora*.

The height to which the aurora extends has never been established. At times it can be several hundred miles upward, and it is rarely less than 50 miles.

The aurora borealis, or northern lights

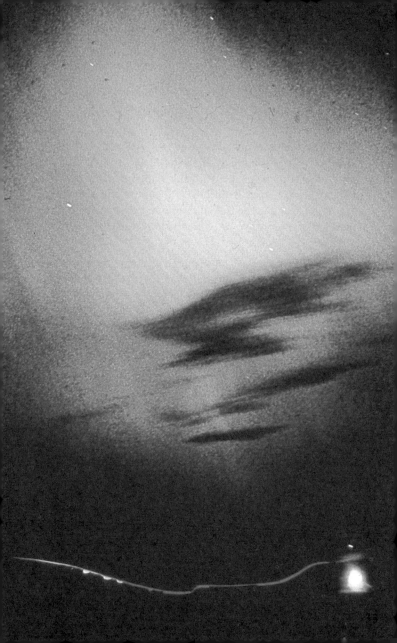

Mountains and glaciers

Apart from volcanoes, many of the mountains we see today were created when the Earth's crust lifted upward and either folded or warped. The Himalayas are an example of intense folding raised up over tens of millions of years.

The great mountain chains under the Atlantic and Pacific Oceans are bigger than any that rise from dry land. The mountains beneath the waters of the Atlantic extend 10,000 miles from north to south, and are about 500 miles wide at their base. Here and there their highest peaks rise above the sea to form islands, such as the Azores.

Many mountains on land are high enough to have snow and ice on them all the time, for the temperature of the air falls 3.6°F for every 1,000 feet above sea level.

Mount Fuji, Japan

On some mountains the winter snowfall is so heavy that glaciers form. Such glaciers usually move very slowly. The Beardmore Glacier in Antarctica—the largest in the world—moves less than one yard a day. The glaciers on Greenland move more rapidly—some as much as 60 feet a day.

A glacier in Greenland

Depressions

Over millions of years, Africa and Arabia have gradually been swinging apart. Along the ever-widening rift, valleys, lakes, and seas have formed in a long line, stretching from Lake Malawi in East Africa north to the Sea of Galilee.

During the long slow process, some molten rock from far beneath the Earth's surface has flowed up to heal the wound, sometimes accompanied by volcanic activity. But some of the valleys in the great chain are still very deep. Jericho, for instance, among the hills that slope down to the River Jordan, is 1,000 feet below sea level, because it stands close to the Dead Sea, which is 1,290 feet below sea level and nearly 1,300 feet deep. The River Jordan from the north, and the River Jaib from the south, both flow into the Dead Sea. Though no water flows out, the Dead Sea's level never rises. It is so hot that the water evaporates as fast as it enters, and it contains as much as 26% salt (most sea water has about 3% or 4% salt at most). Nothing lives in the Dead Sea because of the salt and also the sulfur springs that poison it.

Other kinds of depressions occur on the surface of the Earth. One kind occurs when strong winds, blowing across areas of loose dry earth or sand, scoop out deep hollows. The desert region of North Africa is a good example of this. There are a series of depressions that extend west from Cairo. The biggest of them, the Qattara Depression, is 440 feet below sea level.

The Great Lakes and the Baltic Sea are outstanding examples of another kind of depression. At one time North America and Europe were covered by immense ice sheets as much as 8,000 feet thick. The sheer weight of the ice caused *scouring* and *subsidence* (sinking) of the Earth's crust by up to 2,000 feet where the load was greatest. When the ice began to retreat, the crust began to rise again. It is still rising, but many of North America's fresh-water lakes, and places like the Baltic Sea and Hudson Bay, remain as evidence of rebound depressions.

The Dead Sea

Crystals of salt on the shore of the Dead Sea

Jungles

The Amazon River in Brazil

When we talk about a jungle, we usually mean dense equatorial forest. There is no dry season at all in such regions—the rainfall is heavy all year round, between 60 and 100 inches. Temperatures are always high, averaging 75°F all year.

In this warm, humid climate trees grow fast, often reaching 100 feet in height. Under their dense foliage all kinds of forest plants, especially climbers, struggle up to reach the light. Although the tangled mass of the tropical forest is often almost impenetrable, it swarms with all kinds of life. Monkeys, insects, brightly colored birds, and snakes abound.

But for man, the only real routes through the jungle are the large rivers, teeming with fish, snakes, and other dangerous creatures.

Deserts

A desert is any part of the world where the annual rainfall is less than 10 inches. This means that part of the land within the Arctic Circle is a desert, strictly speaking. The rain or snow there falls a little at a time throughout the year, however, instead of in short sharp bursts, so it is more effective. There is also less loss by evaporation than in places we usually think of as deserts.

In a hot desert like the Sahara, far more moisture would be lost by evaporation than could be replaced by rainfall. A person stranded there without shelter would die of heatstroke and dehydration within 48 hours. This is because the hot dry air soaks up the body's moisture like blotting paper.

There is evidence, however, that this vast, monotonous landscape has not always been barren. Rock carvings, cave paintings, stone implements, and other relics of ancient man show that once, thousands of years ago, the Sahara was rich in vegetation.

Burning of forests and overgrazing by cattle, especially goats, may well have helped to bring about the change. Without trees to provide shade, there is nothing to prevent the sun from burning off surface water. Then, as the sand grows hotter and hotter, the few showers that do fall sink uselessly into it. They may even evaporate before reaching the ground. Surprisingly, the desert grows bitter cold at night, because there are no clouds to keep the heat in.

Desert in Tunisia

The Nyiragongo Volcano, in Zaire, in eruption

Volcanoes

A volcano erupting is one of the greatest spectacles in nature. It is also one of the most frightening, because even today, with all the complex instruments now in use, no one can tell just when an eruption will occur.

An eruption is the last part of a strange chain of events. Far beneath the surface of the Earth, there are pockets of steam and gases and molten rock. If there is just the smallest chink or crack in the rock above, the immense pressure at that great depth forces a stream of molten rock, mixed with gases and steam, through the crack. The steam hurtles upward, collecting stones and earth. Then, when it reaches the air, the gases ignite and start to burn, keeping the rocks liquid for a time.

The red-hot liquid rock is called *lava*. When the gases have all burned away, the lava cools, forming a new layer on the surface of the Earth. Some volcanoes are always on the boil, so that the lava continues to build up and spread out all the time. One of these is Mauna Loa in Hawaii, the biggest volcano in the world. It has been boiling over for so long that it is now 31,000 feet high, measured from its base on the seabed.

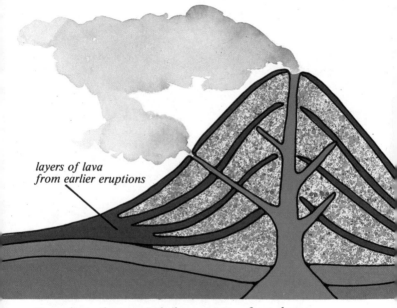

layers of lava from earlier eruptions

Sometimes the escape hole, or vent, of a volcano becomes plugged. This may happen when most of the gases have escaped and the molten rock cools and sets in the escape hole. A volcano that is plugged in this way can stay quiet for a very long time. Eventually, when a strong enough force of gas and steam has built up inside the volcano, the stopper is blown out and there is another eruption.

There are about 500 active volcanoes in the world. Most of them are on the "Ring of Fire" that circles the Pacific Ocean. Outside this ring, there is a chain of volcanoes running almost the length of the Atlantic, from Tristan da Cunha through the Azores to Iceland. Another group, in the Mediterranean, includes Vesuvius, Etna, and Stromboli.

Where volcanoes are found

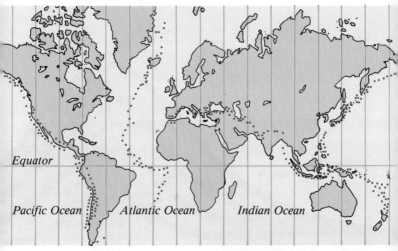

Equator

Pacific Ocean   Atlantic Ocean   Indian Ocean

The most destructive eruption in recorded history, on August 27, 1883, was that of Krakatoa, in the Sunda Strait between Java and Sumatra. The eruption killed 36,000 people and was heard 3,000 miles away. The wall of water raised by the explosion sank dozens of ships. Krakatoa was an island standing 1,400 feet above sea level before the eruption. Not only did the island disappear completely with the eruption, but the ocean bed was excavated to a depth of 1,000 feet.

There are volcanic islands, too, that suddenly appear. In 1929, a new island suddenly came up where Krakatoa had been. It was named Anak Krakatoa—Child of Krakatoa. In 1963, off the coast of Iceland, some fishermen watched as the sea started to boil. Through a vast cloud of steam, the black cone of a volcanic island slowly rose above the surface. Within weeks the new island was 567 feet high and well over a mile long. It was named Surtsey, after a legendary Norse giant.

Old Faithful geyser, in Wyoming.
A geyser is a kind of miniature volcano, from which hot water and steam erupt instead of lava.
Geysers occur in very few parts of the world and are always associated with volcanic activity and cracks in the Earth's surface.

Earthquakes and "tidal" waves

Although no one knows for certain, there are a number of ideas about why earthquakes happen. One of the most widely accepted theories starts with the idea that both the land and the ocean floor rest on a number of separate plates. Each of these plates is made of rock between 40 and 60 miles thick, and floats on molten rock.

The plates move across the globe at between half an inch and 6 inches a year, and sometimes they bang into each other. That is when earthquakes may happen.

There are believed to be several belts on the Earth's surface where plates are moving in this way. One is the "Ring of Fire," already mentioned in connection with volcanoes. It almost encircles the Pacific Ocean. Another is the Alpine Belt, which runs eastward from Spain, along the edges of the Mediterranean Sea, to Turkey, the Himalayas, and the East Indies.

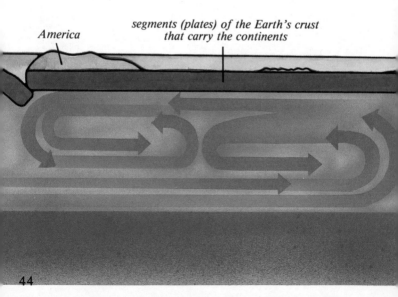

America

segments (plates) of the Earth's crust that carry the continents

The moon is another disturbing factor. Although most people know that the gravitational pull of the moon causes tides, it has another, less well known, effect. As the moon passes overhead, the surface of the land can be pulled up as much as 12 inches. As soon as the moon is on the other side of the Earth, the land sinks back again.

The forces below the surface build up gradually. Then, when the rocks of the Earth's crust above are strained to the breaking point, they suddenly split apart and move, creating waves of vibration—that is, an earthquake.

There are about one million earthquakes every year. In Japan alone, there are as many as three a day. The worst earthquakes release an enormous amount of energy—as much as two and a half times the world's biggest nuclear explosion. On the other hand, some are hardly noticeable.

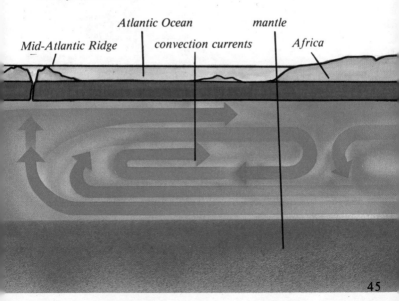

Mid-Atlantic Ridge *Atlantic Ocean* *convection currents* *mantle* *Africa*

A severe earthquake is often followed by a *tsunami*. *Tsunami* is a Japanese word used internationally for the giant waves caused by earthquakes. They are sometimes called "tidal" waves, but they have nothing to do with tides. They are caused by sudden changes in the level of the ocean floor. Although such waves can pass unnoticed in deep water, when they approach shallower water it's a different story. Their energy becomes concentrated, causing waves of terrifying height and destructiveness.

In 1946, an earthquake shook the bed of an ocean deep called the Aleutian Trench, in the North Pacific. The wave it created traveled the 2,250 miles south to Hawaii at an average speed of nearly 493 miles an hour. As it approached the shallower water around the Hawaiian Islands, the wave grew higher.

When it struck the town of Hilo, the front was 45 feet high. It caused more than a hundred million dollars worth of damage, killed 173 people, and injured many more.

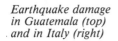

Earthquake damage in Guatemala (top) and in Italy (right)

A meteor seen from Utah

Meteors and shooting stars

On a clear night with no moon, you may sometimes see
a *shooting star*—a spear of light that suddenly appears
and then dies away. It isn't really a star at all; it is a
meteor. Stars are great bodies like the sun, while meteors
are bits of matter, some no bigger than a grain of sand.

On its journey around the sun, the Earth captures
millions of meteors every year. Since they appear with a
certain regularity, it is thought that they may be dust
particles from comets. They travel very fast—perhaps
45 miles a second. So when they strike the atmosphere
protecting the Earth, they are burned up by friction.
Nearly all bits of matter from outer space burn up
completely before reaching the Earth's surface. When
one does reach the Earth, it is called a *meteorite*.

In 1908, meteorites weighing a total of several hundred tons struck an uninhabited part of the Earth in the wastes of Siberia. They devastated 3,088 square miles of forest. The explosion was so violent that it was seen 75 miles away, and the heat was felt for 40 miles. A meteorite that fell in prehistoric times in what is now Arizona left a crater four-fifths of a mile wide and 570 feet deep.

When scientists examined meteorites, they found that some of them were extremely difficult to cut. These particular meteorites contained nine-tenths iron and one-tenth nickel. When iron and nickel are mixed in these proportions, they produce a steel that is hard and tough and is often used as armor plate.

Meteor crater in Arizona

Comets

A comet is made of rock particles, dust, and ice. Like the Earth, it revolves around the sun. The comet has a *coma*, or head, which contains the bright center, or *nucleus*. It may also have a tail of dust or gas (or a mixture of the two). The tail may stretch for millions of miles, always more or less pointing away from the sun.

Only the nucleus is thought to be made of solid matter. In fact, in 1910 the Earth passed through the tail of Halley's comet without any observable effect.

Halley's comet was named after the famous astronomer Edmund Halley. He discovered it in 1705 and established that it appears every 75 years or so. It is known that one of its previous appearances was in 1066, at the time of the Norman invasion of England. The event is recorded in the Bayeux Tapestry.

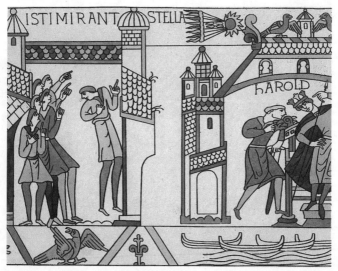

Part of the Bayeux Tapestry showing Halley's Comet

Eclipse seen from Australia   *Eclipse seen from Kenya*

Eclipses

Eclipses of the sun (*solar* eclipses) are of three kinds. First, there is a *total* eclipse, when the sun's light is completely obscured. Then there is a *partial* eclipse, when only part of the sun's surface is hidden. Last, there is an *annular* eclipse, when the central zone of the sun is covered, leaving a ring of light showing.

Total solar eclipses are quite rare. They occur only about once every 350 years at any one place on Earth. The next total eclipse to be seen in the United States will be on July 11, 1991, on the island of Hawaii.

What happens in an eclipse is this: as the moon moves around the Earth, and the Earth moves around the sun, there are times when the three are lined up in such a way that the moon blots out the sun's light, causing an eclipse. The eclipse may last as long as seven and a half minutes.

Ancient civilizations regarded solar eclipses with both fear and awe. Early astronomers, however, may have been able to predict when eclipses would occur. Some people say, for instance, that Stonehenge, in England, may have been constructed as a calendar, and as a system for predicting eclipses and other astronomical events.

The moon receives its light from the sun, so a *lunar* eclipse (eclipse of the moon) takes place when the Earth passes between the sun and the moon.

Index